This Walker book
belongs to:

For Milo Lorcan
and Augusta

First published 2012 by Walker Books Ltd
87 Vauxhall Walk, London SE11 5HJ

This edition published 2013

2 4 6 8 10 9 7 5 3 1

© 2012 Jessica Spanyol

The right of Jessica Spanyol to be identified as author/illustrator of
this work has been asserted by her in accordance with the
Copyright, Designs and Patents Act 1988

This book has been typeset in Typography of Coop

Printed in China

British Library Cataloguing in Publication Data:
a catalogue record for this book is available
from the British Library

ISBN 978-1-4063-4416-5

www.walker.co.uk

MY MUM *is BEAUTiFUL

JESSICA SPANYOL

WALKER BOOKS

AND SUBSIDIARIES

LONDON · BOSTON · SYDNEY · AUCKLAND

My Mum is beautiful because she likes my pictures.

My Mum is beautiful because she helps me sweep up.

My Mum is beautiful because she has my toys in her bath.

My Mum is beautiful because she lets me jump in puddles.

My Mum is beautiful because she has tea with teddy.

My Mum is beautiful because she snuggles up with me.

My Mum is beautiful because she takes me to the café.

My Mum is beautiful because we go shopping together.

My Mum is beautiful because she feeds the ducks with me.

My Mum is beautiful because she laughs when I wear her slippers.

My Mum is beautiful because she really loves me.

My Mum is the most beautiful
Mum in the whole world.

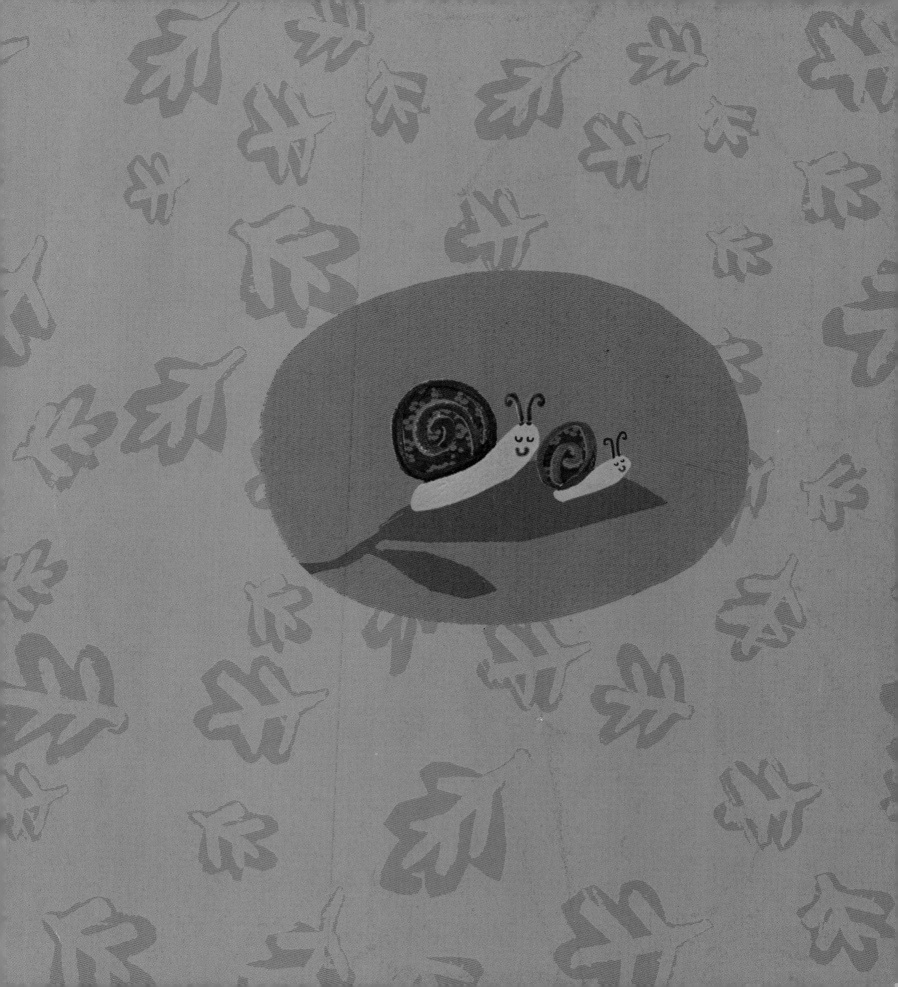

Jessica Spanyol has created numerous children's books, including a series about Carlo the inquisitive giraffe. She has had many different jobs as an artist – in many different places, from schools to theatres – but "Making books for children," she says, "is by far the best fun." Jessica lives in London with her husband and three children.

Other books by Jessica Spanyol:

ISBN 978-0-7445-8934-4

ISBN 978-0-7445-9491-1

ISBN 978-0-7445-9831-5

ISBN 978-1-84428-512-9

The companion volume to My Mum is Beautiful...

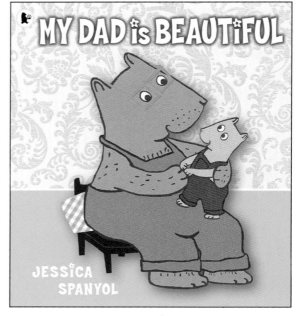

ISBN 978-1-4063-3831-7

Available from all good booksellers
www.walker.co.uk